Samuel French Acting Edition

How To Get
Into Buildings

by Trish Harnetiaux

SAMUELFRENCH.COM   SAMUELFRENCH.CO.UK

FOR PRODUCTION ENQUIRIES

UNITED STATES AND CANADA
Info@SamuelFrench.com
1-866-598-8449

UNITED KINGDOM AND EUROPE
Plays@SamuelFrench.co.uk
020-7255-4302

Each title is subject to availability from Samuel French, depending upon country of performance. Please be aware that *HOW TO GET INTO BUILDINGS* may not be licensed by Samuel French in your territory. Professional and amateur producers should contact the nearest Samuel French office or licensing partner to verify availability.

MUSIC USE NOTE

Licensees are solely responsible for obtaining formal written permission from copyright owners to use copyrighted music in the performance of this play and are strongly cautioned to do so. If no such permission is obtained by the licensee, then the licensee must use only original music that the licensee owns and controls. Licensees are solely responsible and liable for all music clearances and shall indemnify the copyright owners of the play(s) and their licensing agent, Samuel French, against any costs, expenses, losses and liabilities arising from the use of music by licensees. Please contact the appropriate music licensing authority in your territory for the rights to any incidental music.

IMPORTANT BILLING AND CREDIT REQUIREMENTS

If you have obtained performance rights to this title, please refer to your licensing agreement for important billing and credit requirements.

HOW TO GET INTO BUILDINGS was was first produced by New Georges (Susan Bernfield, Producing Artistic Director; Jaynie Saunders Tiller, Managing Director; Sarah Cameron Sunde, Deputy Artistic Director) at The Brick in Brooklyn, New York, on December 3, 2015. The performance was directed by Katherine Brook, with set design by Katherine Brook with Josh Smith, lighting design by Josh Smith, sound design by Chris Giarmo, costume design by Normandy Sherwood, and choreography by David Neumann. The production manager was Rob Signom, the production stage manager was Jaimie Van Dyke, and the assistant director was Leigh Walter. The cast was as follows:

LUCY MASERATI	Kristine Haruna Lee
ROGER SAUVIGNON	Jacob A. Ware
ETHAN CAMBABERT & THE WAITER & DOCTOR/ WAITER ONE	Jess Barbagallo
DAPHNE PIERRE-PONT & DOCTOR/WAITER TWO	Stephanie Weeks
NICK NOVA-SCOTIA & DOCTOR/WAITER THREE	Mike Iveson
MRS. REINHARDT & DOCTOR/WAITER FOUR	Tina Shepard

CHARACTERS

LUCY MASERATI – She's totally game/cautiously evolving

ROGER SAUVIGNON – He's a bit self-absorbed/yet earnest

ETHAN CAMBABERT
& THE WAITER
& DOCTOR/WAITER ONE – The storyteller/confident/dead serious

DAPHNE PIERRE-PONT
& DOCTOR/WAITER TWO – Easily annoyed/aware/dead serious

NICK NOVA-SCOTIA
& DOCTOR/WAITER THREE – Restless and easily offended/dead serious

MRS. REINHARDT
& DOCTOR/WAITER FOUR – Wisely ambivalent/dead serious

AUTHOR'S NOTES

STRUCTURE

The structure is inspired by an Exploded View.

EXPLODED VIEW: an abstract view of an object which allows the viewer to see itemized parts individually, but still understand how they relate to each other as a complete whole.

For example: here's an example of an exploded view of a bicycle. But don't be confused, this play is not about a bicycle, this is just an example of something in exploded view form.

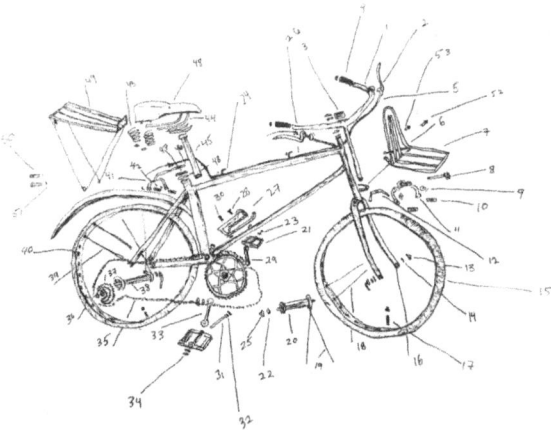

SOUND

This play should be full of sound, as indicated. It's important to include as part of the tissue connecting the Exploded View structure.

DOCTORS/WAITERS

Everyone except for the characters of Lucy and Roger are double cast as a Doctor/Waiter. Their short scenes should never be precious with overemphasis on the language. They should be dirty, messy passages that fuse confusion and confidence, through the manipulation of tone and pitch. Ethan is more a Waiter than a Doctor.

Diverse casting is more than encouraged.

***

For JW

(In the dark, there is the sound of a car accident.)

(Two figures are strangely clumped together. Oh, it's four figures, but looks like two.)

(A few moments of silence, then the crickets resume.)

ROGER & NICK. Don't take your finger off of my –

LUCY & DAPHNE. Your what?

ROGER & NICK. NO! Don't even think of removing your hand from my –

LUCY & DAPHNE. Leg?

ROGER & NICK. No –

LUCY & DAPHNE. Thigh?

ROGER & NICK. Whatever you do, I'd appreciate it if you –

LUCY & DAPHNE. Didn't remove my hand –

ROGER & NICK. I'll bleed –

LUCY & DAPHNE. Red. You'll bleed red –

ROGER & NICK. I'll bleed out.

> *(Beat.)*

> *(Then, overlapping –)*

Are you –

LUCY & DAPHNE. I think so.

ROGER & NICK. Alright. Is it bad –

LUCY & DAPHNE. I can't see it –

ROGER & NICK. – can you see it?

LUCY & DAPHNE. No. It's too dark.

***

> *(Shift.)*

(The **DOCTOR/WAITERS** *enter. They are called* **DOCTOR/WAITERS** *because it is often unclear whether they are* **DOCTORS** *or* **WAITERS***.)*

DOCTOR/WAITER ONE. What part is it missing?

DOCTOR/WAITER TWO. No heart –

DOCTOR/WAITER THREE. Very upset –

DOCTOR/WAITER FOUR. There was a curve –

DOCTOR/WAITER TWO. There is a mark on her face, she is missing an arm, she woke up and it was gone.

DOCTOR/WAITER THREE. No left knee.

DOCTOR/WAITER TWO. Something about a car –

DOCTOR/WAITER ONE. A bashed in cheekbone.

DOCTOR/WAITER TWO. Something about a bar –

DOCTOR/WAITER FOUR. Steel rod through the right shoulder blade –

DOCTOR/WAITER ONE. The truck carried fish.

DOCTOR/WAITER THREE. Small patch of scalp missing at base of neck.

DOCTOR/WAITER ONE. Snapper we believe –

DOCTOR/WAITER TWO. A curve in the road.

DOCTOR/WAITER ONE. Red snapper.

DOCTOR/WAITER THREE. Yes, a curve –

DOCTOR/WAITER TWO. The curve was un/avoidable.

ALL. Unavoidable.

DOCTOR/WAITER ONE. Neck? Fried.

DOCTOR/WAITER TWO. Wrist?

DOCTOR/WAITER ONE. With a hollandaise.

DOCTOR/WAITER THREE. Heart?

DOCTOR/WAITER FOUR. Heart?

DOCTOR/WAITER THREE. There are two hearts.

DOCTOR/WAITER FOUR. Two hearts.

DOCTOR/WAITER ONE. Artichoke heart.

DOCTOR/WAITER THREE. One and then the other.

DOCTOR/WAITER FOUR. That's the two –

DOCTOR/WAITER ONE. Oh, yes.

DOCTOR/WAITER TWO. Oh, yep.

DOCTOR/WAITER FOUR. Broken artichoke heart bone.

DOCTOR/WAITER THREE. One is outside the –

DOCTOR/WAITER ONE. Yes.

DOCTOR/WAITER FOUR. Does it bother her when –

DOCTOR/WAITER ONE. YES.

DOCTOR/WAITER THREE. That's a shame.

DOCTOR/WAITER ONE. A shame.

DOCTOR/WAITER TWO. Shame.

DOCTOR/WAITER THREE. It's shameful.

DOCTOR/WAITER FOUR. Absolutely –

(They exit or something.)

***

(Shift.)

(A bright wash. The lobby of a convention center. There is wall-to-wall carpeting, a few large plants, and a bench. Some convention center lobby music.)

(A normal-seeming woman, LUCY, is sitting quietly eating her lunch with chopsticks – it's a delicious looking Bento Box. ROGER approaches and sits nearby. Something about him indicates his hero-worship of Marvel Comic's Silver Surfer, perhaps it's his backpack and the small silver surfboard peeking out the top. He opens the backpack and pulls out a huge – too huge, really – bag of chips.)

ROGER. Huh – chopsticks, nice.

LUCY. Excuse me?

ROGER. Chopsticks. Nice.

LUCY. Would you, would you like one, or, some? I have extra.

ROGER. Sure, thanks.

(*LUCY hands him some chopsticks.* **ROGER** *gratefully accepts and opens the bag of chips. He breaks the chopsticks apart and tries to lift chips one by one to his mouth. He is unsuccessful.*)

(*He drops a chopstick. She smiles.*)

***

(*A muffled phone rings from* **LUCY**'*s bag.*)

(*She removes her cell phone and listens.*)

(**MRS. REINHARDT**'*s voice.*)

MRS. REINHARDT. Are you a first time caller?

(*She turns slightly away from* **ROGER**.)

LUCY. Yes.

MRS. REINHARDT. Well, we're thrilled you called in.

LUCY. Yes.

MRS. REINHARDT. Are you a long time listener?

LUCY. Yes.

MRS. REINHARDT. It's people like you that keep us alive.

LUCY. Yes.

MRS. REINHARDT. People like you.

That have always been meaning to call, have never quite gotten around to it, but now find themselves in a position to *help*.

LUCY. I suppose.

MRS. REINHARDT. You sound like you're in love.

(*Beat.* **LUCY** *glances at* **ROGER**, *but briefly.*)

You sound just like a person that's made a recent big decision to let someone into your life and stop being so selfish and I bet, now, you've been drinking a little less – am I right?

(*Beat.*)

I can tell by your complexion. One day, you'll look over and he'll be sitting there.

(LUCY glances briefly at ROGER again, but differently.)

You'll be sitting *here*,

and he'll be sitting *there*.

LUCY. I'll be sitting *here*.

MRS. REINHARDT. He'll have come from a distant galaxy. He doesn't know it's you. All this not a minute too soon is what I say...everyone knows you were about to disappear, without a trace, never to be seen –

(Click. LUCY closes the phone and turns back toward ROGER.)

***

(LUCY watches ROGER eat his chips with the chopsticks and study a set of note cards balanced on one knee.)

(She...reflects on her awful luck with love as...)

(ETHAN enters. His iPod is still on, but his headphones are around his neck, so we can still faintly hear the awfulness of a U2 song coming from it.*)

ETHAN. Guess how many cats I have?

LUCY. Oh, I couldn't –

ETHAN. Just guess, really, there are no stupid guesses.

(They share a smile.)

LUCY. I don't know...a hundred.

---

*A license to produce *How To Get Into Buildings* does not include a performance license for any U2 song. The publisher and author suggest that the licensee contact ASCAP or BMI to ascertain the music publisher and contact such music publisher to license or acquire permission for performance of the song. If a license or permission is unattainable for a U2 song the licensee may not use the song in *How To Get Into Buildings* but may create an original composition in a similar style. For further information, please see Music Use Note on page 3.

ETHAN. That's a stupid guess. Did you even really think about it before you blurted that shit out? Think about what you already know about me. You know I live in an apartment, right?

LUCY. (*Quietly.*) I was jok–

ETHAN. You know I was laid off last year and no matter how hard I try, no matter how many mornings I get up before dawn and go looking for a job, etc, etc, ETC – you know I wasn't able to find one until last month.

> (*Beat.*)

Correct? Am I correct?

LUCY. I'm sorry.

> (*Rises.*)

I should go –

ETHAN. Just sit your stupid idiot self down. I'm only teasing. *Stupid.* I have seventeen cats. Want to hear their names? Toshi, Boshi, Noshi, Floshi, Baby, Nabi, Wabi, Labi, Sabertooth, Clementine, Botchi, Potchi, Lotchi, Zotchi, Melonball, Zucchini Face, and Labia.

> (*He smiles and walks on.*)

* * *

> (**NICK** and **DAPHNE** are at the diner looking at very large menus.)
>
> (*Terrible Muzak plays.*)
>
> (**DAPHNE** wears a purple scarf.)
>
> (**ETHAN** enters as **THE WAITER**.)

THE WAITER. I'm afraid to say. We are…out of the fish. It was…Snapper. In case you…were wondering. Red Snapper.

NICK.	**DAPHNE**.
That's okay.	Whatever.

> (*Beat.*)

THE WAITER. Well, okay…Correction. I *was* afraid to say "We are out of the fish." But –

(*Quick smile.*)

– it seems you're taking it well, so I'm a little less, a little less afraid. I'll be slightly less intimidated, and less afraid, telling my next table. Thank you. I thank you for that. A learning curve, that's what I just went through, or around, it is a curve and all, or…I know – let me take *this* little moment to say that is a very, very nice scarf. The purples and rose hues and such. I believe my mother had a scarf like that…

(*Brief smile.*)

Oh god. Wait…

(*Horror.*)

I'm sorry…I'm having this terrible memory of that scarf now…

(**THE WAITER** *backs away, terrified.*)

(**DAPHNE** *looks confused, but then, like, normal.*)

(**NICK** *looks at the menu.*)

(*Awful Muzak continues.*)

NICK. So…what are you going to get?

DAPHNE. Hmmmm.

NICK. This menu is, ah, large.

DAPHNE. Yes. So many, so many…omelets.

NICK. And waffles. I'm mostly interested in waffles.

DAPHNE. Wow.

(*Snorts.*)

That's surprising.

(*Beat.*)

I just remember how much you liked the omelets last time…

NICK. I know.

DAPHNE. You made a point to get an *omelet* last time.

(The Muzak starts to get louder.)

NICK. I did.

(NICK searches for the origin of the awful Muzak –)

DAPHNE. Did that whole thing with your *hat* and the menu and –

NICK. *(To no one, but to everyone.)* JESUS! Can you turn this SHIT down??

(The Muzak stops.)

DAPHNE. *Nick.*

(Beat.)

NICK. It's just that the waffles seem more, I don't know, appropriate today. Now. Today. *Waffle day.*

DAPHNE. Appropriate?

NICK. I…guess.

(Beat.)

Are you going to have juice?

DAPHNE. *JUICE??*

NICK. Yeah.

DAPHNE. *NO.*

NICK. *Daphne.*

DAPHNE. I had some at home.

NICK. *YOU DID??*

DAPHNE. You *watched me* –

NICK. I never saw –

DAPHNE. – drink it straight from the fridge.

(Under breath.)

Jesus.

NICK. *("Acting" confused.)* You knew we were coming here? Why would you –

DAPHNE. Don't act so *confused.*

NICK. You could have waited.

DAPHNE. I like a belt of it. A belt of juice in the morning.

NICK. A what?

DAPHNE. A belt of JUICE.

NICK. That doesn't even make sense, a belt...

    (Beat.)

    (Sigh.)

  Are you going to get home fries?

DAPHNE. Yeah.

NICK. I think I'll get a belt of them.

    (Beat.)

DAPHNE. What's wrong with you?

    (Beat.)

NICK. I'm hungry.

  Really, I want a belt of home fries.

DAPHNE. Jesus.

***

    *(**LUCY** and **ROGER**, as before.)*

    *(**ROGER** has a piece of chip between his chopsticks.)*

    *(**LUCY** pops a California roll in her mouth.)*

LUCY. I like your surfboard.

ROGER. Yeah?

LUCY. Yeah.

ROGER. Silver Surfer.

    *(**LUCY** has no idea what he is talking about.)*

LUCY. Oh yeah? Cool.

ROGER. Norrin Radd.

LUCY. Excuse me?

ROGER. You a Norrin Radd fan?

LUCY. Yeah.../yep.

ROGER. Cool. Comic Con?

LUCY. What?

ROGER. You here for Comic Con?

LUCY. No, I'm here with the other convention.
Huh.

ROGER. You are?

LUCY. Yep.

>   *(Holding up her Bento Box.)*

Lunch break.

>   *(They smile.)*

* * *

>   *(The sound of rain.)*
>
>   (**ETHAN** *is reading a passage from his new
>   book,* The Car Accident. *The cover is extremely
>   violent.)*

ETHAN. "– and she was whispering in his ear that he was
either a doctor *OR* a waiter. That it was *confusing.* That he
had hollandaise on his *sleeve,* but blood on his *cuff,* so
she couldn't tell. He smelled like Neosporin *and* garlic.
She wasn't sure why at the time, but it was absolutely
necessary for Daphne to find out."

>   *(A loud clap of thunder.* **ETHAN** *turns the page.)*

"*Chapter Thirty-Nine.* On a sunny afternoon, Daphne
shot Nick after brunch. There had been an argument
at a diner; she was surprised he wanted waffles when all
he could talk about the last time they'd eaten there was
how goddamn good the omelets had been. He *couldn't
believe* she'd already had juice earlier that morning, she
knew they were going for brunch, she could have given
him the courtesy of waiting."

>   (**LUCY** *cautiously enters. She carries a red purse
>   and sits in an empty chair.)*

"For *weeks* she'd had to listen about that omelet. The
perfect amount of butter it was cooked in, the freshness
of the cheese, the perfection of the spinach inside – not

too slimy, just crunchy enough to let him know it was fresh and had been picked that morning, then driven to the city at what many would still call the middle of the night.

This made Daphne want to kill herself. And Nick."

(**DAPHNE** *enters and sits.*)

"So, she bought a gun.

At least it was the shape of a gun, but smelled like chocolate. For hours she would stand in front of the mirror watching herself hold it. Staring at her reflection as she raised it up and put it in her mouth. She could practically taste the crushed up peanuts and thin layer of caramel as her lips closed around the barrel, biting into it.

See, Nick was a chef, and couldn't look at anything without immediately trying to find different ways to either eat it, or cook it. And now, Daphne couldn't either."

DAPHNE. *(Barely audible.) Jesus.*

(*A phone starts ringing, only* **LUCY** *appears to hear it.*)

(**LUCY** *realizes it's in her bag and tries to muffle the noise. It's not making much of a difference and she tries to sit on it without drawing too much attention to herself as* **ETHAN** *continues reading.*)

ETHAN. "He would see a flower and wonder how he was going to fill the petals with cheese. His mind already making a light sauce from the stem, mixing diced Amish garlic and organic cow tears. He would spend hours contemplating which would be best, to serve this new dish on an antique plate bought at the flea market in San Telmo or a lopsided plate of his own creation that he had made as a child, that he had glazed in the art room with the other children, the summer he was sent to the camp in the mountains with the other boys that had been bad. The question was, and this was always the question, which would his mother like best?"

(*The ringing has not stopped.*)

(*The rain has not stopped.*)

(**LUCY** *brings her red purse back onto her lap.*)

***

(**LUCY** *swivels slightly so she's facing away from* **ETHAN** *and gently pulls an old-school phone receiver – complete with curly cord – awkwardly from her bag. During the following,* **ETHAN** *continues to read [but with no sound] and* **DAPHNE** *continues to listen and occasionally shake her head in response.*)

(**LUCY** *glances around and whispers –*)

LUCY. Hello…

MRS. REINHARDT. Are you a first time caller?

LUCY. Yes.

MRS. REINHARDT. Are you a long time listener?

LUCY. Yes.

MRS. REINHARDT. Well, we're thrilled you called in.

LUCY. I'd been meaning to call.

MRS. REINHARDT. People like you have always been meaning to call. But the problem is, you don't. You sound like you've got a good head on your shoulders. You sound like you can spot trouble a mile away and let me tell you that's no small skill young lady.

LUCY. I'm just calling to –

MRS. REINHARDT. You're just calling to hear me out, now listen closely.

You'll be walking along one day and it'll start raining.

You'll have forgotten your coat,

your hat,

your umbrella.

You'll see a diner and you'll duck in for cover.
Then you're in a booth with steaming coffee,
a wet newspaper near your elbow,
some spilled sugar.
Before you know it you're off balance,
off kilter,
a curve in the road,
a *learning* curve,
the curvature of the spine –

LUCY. There will be an accident –

MRS. REINHARDT. – which we're more than happy to simply deduct from your account each month. No need to remember, no need to pull out that checkbook or lick that envelope. No need to search the couch cushions for a stamp, slicing your palm with the steak knife you pull out instead. It will be automatic.

LUCY.	MRS. REINHARDT.
Clockwork.	Clockwork.

LUCY. A small donation will be fine. Each month. Ten dollars.

MRS. REINHARDT. Eleven dollars?

> (**LUCY** *really doesn't want to do eleven dollars, but she does.*)

LUCY. Eleven dollars…

> (**LUCY** *places the receiver back in her bag.*)

> (**ETHAN** *is in the last moments of his reading.*)

ETHAN. "– and she was screaming, 'HEY – DON'T I KNOW YOU FROM THE HOUSE OF PUDDING?'
But it was too late…she had already rounded the corner and disappeared. (*Gone.*)
She licked some drops of blood off her hand, then smiled, realizing it was chocolate."

***

*(**LUCY** and **ROGER** eating lunch.)*

ROGER. So, you're here for the *other* convention?

LUCY. I come every year.

ROGER. I can't believe you're / here with the *other* –

LUCY. Well, I guess that's not true, I missed…last year.

ROGER. You don't seem the type?

LUCY. Type?

ROGER. You look…put together.

LUCY. Thanks, I guess?

(He gestures generally at her.)

ROGER. Whichever one it is, it's like I can't even tell.

LUCY. Excuse me?

ROGER. Like, BOTH of your legs look REAL.

LUCY. They *are.*

ROGER. Then, my god, NICE job on the arms!

LUCY. What?

ROGER. So cool, how they move at the elbow and everything –

LUCY. As opposed to?

ROGER. And your hands, did they take that skin from your *thigh*? It's so skin-like and –

*(**LUCY** sets down her Bento Box.)*

LUCY. I'm sorry, what's your name?

ROGER. Roger.

LUCY. Roger –

ROGER. What's yours? Wait – let me guess! I'm really good at guessing names, I know that's, er, odd, but I really *like* to do it. Do you mind?

LUCY. Roger –

ROGER. Wait! Before I guess, you're not…a warrior princess right? This one time, wo-ah, *this,* she, was –

LUCY. What convention do you think I'm here for?

ROGER. Portia? No. Juliana? No...Like do you have a small-boys-name-girls-name-type-thing? Shane?

LUCY. No.

ROGER. Dalia?

LUCY. What convention do you think I'm here for?

ROGER. The Prosthetic...Limb Convention...? Probably / not.

LUCY. Probably not.

> *(She smiles.)*

I think there are like four conventions here.

ROGER. Oh.

> *(Beat.)*

LUCY. Lu/cy –

ROGER. LUCY!

> **(LUCY** *is unclear if* **ROGER** *wants credit for "guessing" her name...)*
>
> *(She holds her hand out to him.)*

LUCY. Touch it.

> **(ROGER** *holds his hand up helplessly.)*

ROGER. *Mustard.*

LUCY. Lick it off.

ROGER. Excuse me?

LUCY. Wipe it off.

> *(She hands him a napkin.)*
>
> *(He wipes the mustard off.)*
>
> *(She holds her hand out again.)*
>
> *(He takes it.)*

Skin like?

> *(They hold their hands together for a moment.)*

ROGER. Very, very skin like.

***

(**NICK** *and* **DAPHNE**, *still at the diner.*)

NICK. I brought you something.

DAPHNE. Uh-huh.

(**NICK** *sets a case between them on the table.*)

(**DAPHNE** *snorts, then smiles.*)

Where did you find them –

NICK. I kept them.

DAPHNE. No you *didn't* –

NICK. Kept 'em.

(*Smiles.*)

Surprised aren't you?

DAPHNE. No –

NICK. You love it when I surprise y–

DAPHNE. I hate it.

(**THE WAITER** *appears.*)

THE WAITER. Nice guns.

(**NICK** *touches his own arm, caresses it.*)

NICK. Thanks. Don't worry –

THE WAITER. Sir –

NICK. – they're not loaded.

THE WAITER. I'm afraid we don't –

NICK. I didn't see any *signs* –

THE WAITER. We have a No Fire Arms Policy.

NICK. As you should, as you should.

(**THE WAITER** *exits.*)

(*That terrible Muzak sneaks back on, but softly. Neither notice, but if* **NICK** *had noticed, he probably would have liked it this time.*)

(**DAPHNE** *gets distracted by a sign past* **NICK***'s head.*)

DAPHNE. Oh god –

NICK. What?

DAPHNE. Oh my god.

NICK. WHAT?

DAPHNE. Of course

NICK. *Jesus.* WHAT?

DAPHNE. CASH ONLY.

NICK. No –

DAPHNE. It's cash only.

NICK. Since when? GOD.

DAPHNE. This place is *cash only?*

NICK. Why do you always take me to cash –

DAPHNE. *I didn't know.*

NICK. You should've checked –

DAPHNE. I can't do *EVERYTHING.*

NICK. It's okay –

DAPHNE. *Pisses me off.*

NICK. *IT'S FINE.*

DAPHNE. How many dishes did we even have?

NICK. Dishes?

DAPHNE. *Dishes.*

> (**NICK** *sighs.*)

NICK.	**DAPHNE.**
Minty Lamb Sliders.	Three sliders each, times two, you didn't eat one –

NICK. *MINTY LAMB SLIDERS.* One dish. ONE dish.

DAPHNE. *(Panicking.)* Well what are going to do, I don't have cash –

NICK. It's okay –

DAPHNE. We should have split an –

NICK. I got it.

DAPHNE. *You* have cash.

> (*Beat.*)

NICK. I have cash.

DAPHNE. YOU have CASH.

NICK. I have cash.

DAPHNE. YOU have cash.

NICK. Yes.

DAPHNE. Well.
  Alright.

> (**DAPHNE** *pulls the case toward her as* **NICK** *reaches for his wallet.*)

***

> (**ETHAN**, *as before, reading from his book* The Car Accident.*)
>
> (*The rain.*)
>
> (**DAPHNE** *adjusts her seating to become a captive member of his audience.*)
>
> (**NICK** *counts money from his wallet.*)

ETHAN. "*Chapter One Hundred Thirty Four – The Bento Box.*
  Lucy would ONLY eat lunch out of a Bento Box.
  It was no secret that the true allure of the Bento Box was in how each item, each separate *piece* of lunch, was in its own compartment – guaranteeing that everything retained its own unique flavor.
  The chicken teriyaki.
  The little bit of salad.
  The dumplings.
  The small California roll.
  Delicious.
  And separate.
  One needn't worry about the purity of the bite for example, and Lucy appreciated this.
  This was futile to Roger whose natural born state is slight paranoia. When this is directed at food, it materializes in his belief that everything contains bones. That flattening his food with anything nearby is the only solution – a fork, a glass, a shoe.

Flatten.

Cut.

Examine.

Eat.

He was fond of the story that once, when he was small, he found chicken bones inside his artichoke heart at a vegan restaurant. No one choked, but it was enough to provoke Roger to throw a fit – turning the table-tops upside down, throwing plates against the wall and ultimately breaking his pelvic bone, which put him on bed rest for the three months leading up to his ninth birthday.

Later, he'd trace this incident as one of the most shaping of his childhood. It was then that he lay, propped up with pillows, and opened issue one of *The Silver Surfer: Escape to Terror!* He was hooked from the first caption:

'Safely hidden atop the towering Himalayas, in a lonely, long-lost land, tortured by his own anguished thoughts, sits the Silver Surfer!'

They were the most real words he had ever read."

(**ETHAN** *continues to read, but we don't hear him.*)

***

(**ROGER** *and* **LUCY** *are still having lunch.*)

ROGER. It's such a hard question, right? What do I like to do…

(**ROGER** *reaches over into her Bento Box.*)

LUCY. Are you reaching into my Bento Box?

(*He pops a California roll in his mouth.*)

ROGER. So. Hmm. I like… I like to bury things? Maybe that's the wrong answer. I like to take things and dig holes for them, then wrap them in some kind of casing or coating or plastic and then lay them really gently in the earth and cover it back up with dirt or rock or sand

– it, of course, *absolutely* depends where I am. I have *seriously* buried all sorts of things, like fish and –

> *(Laughs it off.)*

It's ridiculous. Sorry, usually I don't tell this sort of thing to someone I just met.

I should –

I should change the...

So...

If you had a boat what would you name it?

LUCY. I'm not –

ROGER. Really, I'm polling people. Say you had a boat.

LUCY. A sailboat?

ROGER. A tugboat, a sailboat, whatever – now, name it.

LUCY. Sun/shine –

ROGER. SUNDAY!

> *(Beat.)*

ROGER. I'd call my boat *Zenn-La*.

LUCY. Cool.

ROGER. Or *Shalla-Bal*. Which one sounds better?

LUCY. *Huh?*

ROGER. So, I guess *Shalla-Bal*, right?

LUCY. *Sunshine-Shalla-Bal!*

> *(Beat.)*
>
> *(It feels strangely too soon for* **LUCY** *to marry their boat names...)*

ROGER. Ok, forget the boat. Don't think I'm weird. Could you help –

LUCY. I'd love too.

> *(She answered that a little too quickly, but* **ROGER** *doesn't mind.)*
>
> *(He grabs the note cards he's been studying.)*

ROGER. I have this presentation...I could show –

LUCY. Absolutely.

(Ugh! She did it again.)

ROGER. I need to warn you that I'm really weird about feedback.

LUCY. Weird...about feedback?

ROGER. Criticism. Feedback. Like just *censor* yourself. I'm not one of those guys that "likes it straight," at least not right away. For now, just tell me it's astonishing or something, okay?

LUCY. Sure –

ROGER. And, I'm not saying that I'm going to get to know you better, it's just that I'm not sure I could take it if you, like, yelled at me –

LUCY. That's not going to happen.

ROGER. – don't get me started about why I quit the wrestling team –

LUCY. There's no way I'll yell at you.

ROGER. That's what *he* said.

(He's nervous.)

LUCY. I'm incredibly selfish.

ROGER. No –

LUCY. You're bad at criticism. I'm selfish, I'm terrible, it's something I'm working on. Actively. See?

ROGER. No way.

LUCY. I'm actively working on it. It's not...natural.

*(***ROGER** *smiles.)*

ROGER. Don't try to make me...more comfortable.

LUCY. I'm not! That would be *giving* of me, and as I just said, I'm not a very giving person. So.

(He smiles again. He stands.)

(He clears his throat and glances at his note cards.)

ROGER. Imagine there's these slides behind me with images and stuff, really creative images that enhance the words, and I'll play this song then –

LUCY. Just start –

ROGER. Okay.

Good afternoon Ladies and Gentlemen, Superheroes and Lords of the Underworld. Without further *adieu*, I shall begin:

> *(He holds the first note card. It's like he's about to start…then doesn't.)*

…Or, maybe, I shouldn't, you know, *blow my wad.*

> *(Hmm.)*

That's a disgusting phrase.

I want to acknowledge that I know.

That I'm aware.

That you are probably thinking –

LUCY.	**ROGER.**
You seem a bit wound up –	– that I have just used a disgusting phrase.

LUCY. You're making a classic mistake right now: thinking too much about other people.

I have a, ah, a friend that used to do that all the time…

She'd get all freaked out that no one could hear her when she spoke.

Started SHOUTING ALL THE TIME!

Like her ears hadn't popped from that stupid, *expensive,* return *flight* from fucking Bolivia.

Awful.

Have you ever traveled with friends and loved ones in South America?

Don't answer that.

Don't.

Don't try to have like your entire life experiences in every single moment.

Just…take a breath.

Tell me about what you're thinking…

ROGER. Like casually?

LUCY. You don't have to actually do it.

ROGER. Ahh, that's interesting.

LUCY. Speak from the heart?

ROGER. I like that.

> (ROGER *takes a moment, trying to really locate his heart.*)

Okay.

> (*He holds the first note card.*)

The opening is the most important – you only have seconds to get them, so I'm going to start with a BANG. A little interaction-scenario-thing about: How-To-Demand-Access.

LUCY. I'm riveted.

> (ROGER *smiles and glances down and shuffles to the second note card.*)

ROGER. Okay, cool. Next, it's important to relate directly with each person. I'm…I'm trying to speak their *language* and create a sense of…shared-community-type-stuff? How we all fall prey to the same – societal mistakes type-a-thing? Okay.

> (*Third note card.*)

This is where I reinforce that we're – Globally – all in this together. Each and every one of us. Lucy.

LUCY. Yes?

> (*He indicates himself.*)

ROGER. *Roger.*

Global-people-everywhere.

> (*It's like that moment in charades when you're not sure how to do the next thing.*)

Sorry… This is really hard without the visuals.

It's funny, even though they were carefully crafted, I'm only now realizing their importance.

This is *great* actually.

> (*Fourth note card.*)

Okay, I was reading this book about these brothers, and man, they figured it all out. This is a pretty big reveal, so I can't say too much more…But this section is like:

THE BIGGEST MOMENT OF YOUR LIFE

Everything clicking-click-click-click.
Everything firing on all the cylinders,
tail spin,
inverted-thought-revelation-dynamic-portal-to-another-dimension-mind-blowing-fun.
'Cause it's a club.
It is all one big club and you just need an IN.

Man, this is really helpful. Even not saying what I'm really saying is helpful.

    (Fifth note card.)

This last part is like Cap finally joining The Avengers. Sure, everything contributes to the final factor, but the illumination I'm interested in starts with
The Individual.
Thee…self.
Lucy.
Roger.
The doors will just…open.

    (Beat.)

Thank you.

    (LUCY *claps wildly.)*

***

    (ETHAN *is still reading.)*

    (It is still raining.)

ETHAN. "Nick grew up never going to restaurants because his mother couldn't understand what she would describe as a certain *desperateness* to people that just had to assemble in public together. She'd have nightmares of too many arms and legs everywhere."

(Quieter.)

"It didn't matter now.
They were nearing the end."

(Then building.)

"Daphne sees orange juice as an out.
Nick looks at a menu and sees a retirement home brochure.
She sees a salt shaker as a weapon.
He sees a cardboard box wishing for a Bento Box.
Then the daggers and swords melt together and there are two pistols sitting in front of them,
a salt and pepper shaker,
a spoon suspended in air,
a tower of sugar in between.
Maybe a crumpled up napkin,
her fork,
his knife,
the ketchup cap.
Both of them staring at the pistol they have secretly chosen for themselves, knowing they will end up how they always end up –
Isolated in time, unaware of the shift.
Seemingly content but ultimately unsatisfied.
A breeze, some dust, that woman in the rocking chair.
Daphne calmly pushes up the puffy sleeves on her barmaid's dress, assuring she won't snag her thumb on the fabric when her hand rushes to her side.

Words like *eventuality* and *inevitability* – once just high school vocab words – now described the cold feeling of anticipation that was delivered with their breakfast bill."

***

(The Muzak again…)

*(**NICK** brushes something off **DAPHNE**'s shoulder.)*

*(**NICK** picks something off **DAPHNE**'s arm.)*

(He leans in, as if to remove something else from her, but gives up halfway through.)

NICK. What is that?

DAPHNE. What?

NICK. That thing on your sleeve.

DAPHNE. My cuff.

NICK. Uh, no…

DAPHNE. That thing on my sleeve is the *cuff of my sleeve.*

(She looks hard at his face.)

Oh god, what's that?

NICK. What?

DAPHNE. On your FACE.

(He hates it, but he's alarmed.)

NICK. *What is it –*

DAPHNE. *Oh gross –*

NICK. Get it –

DAPHNE. – it's disgusting –

NICK. *– off. Get it off.*

(She grabs at his face, pulling his nose.)

Ow! What are you doing?

DAPHNE. Oh, it's just your stupid nose.

(She laughs.)

NICK. You have *shit* all over yourself.

DAPHNE. Shit.

NICK. *SHIT.*

DAPHNE. *I have shit all over myself?*

NICK. Did you even use a utensil?

*(A spoon flies in and **DAPHNE** catches it as if it's always been in her hand.)*

(**ETHAN** *appears with even more silverware.*)

THE WAITER. Does someone need a utensil? Ma'am?

> (*Beat.*)

Or, sir, perhaps you're craving a root vegetable of some sort?

> (**DAPHNE** *and* **THE WAITER** *smile at each other a little.*)

> (**NICK** *assesses the moment...then deliberately gets up and walks downstage to deliver the following to the audience.*)

NICK. My mother told me that certain vegetables...hated each other.

Radishes fucking can't stand carrots for example.

Or *other* radishes for that matter.

They're competitors.

They *literally* compete.

For the same dip.

Think about it.

Humus.

Think about it.

Shit, baba ganoush?

This is most common with...root vegetables.

...Just hiding in the fucking ground all year.

> (*A long...uncomfortable beat.*)

> (**THE WAITER** *backs away, cradling the water pitcher.*)

***

> (**LUCY** *and* **ROGER** *are sitting as before, maybe a tiny bit closer together.*)

> (**ROGER** *hands* **LUCY** *a small chain.*)

ROGER. This is for you.

LUCY. Thanks. What is it?

ROGER. It's a small chain.

LUCY. Yeah?

ROGER. It's really special.

LUCY. Wow.

ROGER. Yeah.

LUCY. That's cool.

> *(Beat…)*

> *(…And then another beat.)*

ROGER. It's from the Titanic.

LUCY. The Titanic?

ROGER. Right?!

LUCY. *No way!*

ROGER. Yeah, they think that maybe it was in a bathroom…
Like connected to the little rubber stopper that plugs
up the bathtub…the stopper thing.

> *(She inspects the little chain in her hand.)*

LUCY. Huh…

ROGER. That's –

LUCY. Ironic.

ROGER. – what I thought.

LUCY. Hmmm.

> *(Looking closer.)*

ROGER. What?

LUCY. Are you sure this is from the Titanic?

ROGER. What – why?

LUCY. Just like…
are you sure that this is like an "Official Artifact"?

ROGER. Sure.
Yes.

> *(**LUCY** really inspects the chain.)*

LUCY. That's weird.

ROGER. Like, "weird that it's from the Titanic" weird?

LUCY. I...

ROGER. Or –

LUCY. I don't...

ROGER. – it's weird that we just met and I'm giving you a present? Because that's just me, that's just who-I-am. I totally like to give people –

LUCY. I don't think –

> *(Unfortunately, with reserve, she sets the chain down.)*

I don't think...that this chain is from the Titanic, actually.

ROGER. That's what...the guy...

> *(Beat.)*

> *(She almost doesn't...but she picks the chain back up.)*

LUCY. I like the clasp.

> (**ROGER** *is visibly relieved.*)

ROGER. Yeah?

LUCY. You have to look super close, but see here? It's initials –

ROGER. Oh yeah –

LUCY. Someone's initials.

> *(Looks even closer at the chain.)*

Or –

ROGER. How cool is that. Those initials, some poor, lost, probably drown –

LUCY. Oh.

ROGER. I wonder if it had been a gift –

LUCY. No...

ROGER. A present even –

LUCY. Wait...

ROGER. – he got it for her birthday –

LUCY. This is a cat collar.

ROGER. Excuse me?

LUCY. It says... PURR.

> *(Beat.)*

ROGER. Purr?

LUCY. P-U-R-R.

ROGER. Huh, cat collar.

That's like a really weird name. For a cat.

Purr.

Rr.

Can you roll your R's?

LUCY. No.

ROGER. Purrrrrrrrr. Me neither.

***

> *(**ETHAN** reading.)*
>
> *(The rain.)*

ETHAN. "– and as Roger looked at her he was thinking, 'Maybe one day I'll take you to dinner, we'll go to a restaurant, you'll order the fish, I'll have a steak, we'll have wine and laugh and I'll tell you all about the time I broke my pelvic bone when I was nine years old, how I couldn't move from bed for months and that's when I fell in love with the Silver Surfer, that's when I lived on Zenn-La, that's when I would call you Shalla-Bal. That's when I left you, had to leave you to save you. That's when I fought to defend our planet to ensure that you would live. It's always been for you.'"

***

> *(No phone is even ringing.)*
>
> *(**LUCY** takes the phone out of her bag.)*

(She puts it to her ear and listens. Someone picks it up –)

LUCY. I'm a first-time caller –

(We can hear MRS. REINHARDT breathing.)

A long-time listener?

(We can hear MRS. REINHARDT lightly laughing.)

I'm so glad to have finally called in.

MRS. REINHARDT. Finally.

LUCY. Have you –

MRS. REINHARDT. Have you seen the memorial or statue –

LUCY. I'm not sure about the urgency –

MRS. REINHARDT. It's cut from steel with knobs of wood
and plaster handles.
Right there in the park,
just downtown,
it's for everyone. Has a slide.
They sit, immortal, at the foot of a stool,
the end of a bench,
up near the grassy knoll.

LUCY. Do you think it's alright to partially commit to ideas
of grandeur?

MRS. REINHARDT. *Copper.*

LUCY. Is it okay to live in uncertainty?

MRS. REINHARDT. We need to raise the funds,
to polish up the oxidation.

LUCY. Will that fix it?

(MRS. REINHARDT laughs.)

MRS. REINHARDT. If enough money is raised,
it's all forgotten.
That's how it goes,
like forgiveness.

LUCY. How much needs to be, to be given?

MRS. REINHARDT. Enough to do the arms and legs and face and hands and heart.

LUCY. How do they fix the heart –

MRS. REINHARDT. With steam and tools and sweat and love.

LUCY. And they start construction soon?

MRS. REINHARDT. That doesn't matter –

LUCY. Of course not –

MRS. REINHARDT. You don't want to know too much.

LUCY. I don't want to / get ahead of myself.

MRS. REINHARDT. Don't get ahead of yourself.

> *(Beat.)*

Hold please –

> *(Hold music comes on.)*

***

> *(The Hold music becomes bad restaurant Muzak, the same song but a different version.)*

> *(LUCY and ROGER sit with menus.)*

> *(NICK and DAPHNE are near, palpably not speaking.)*

> *(NICK and ROGER are back-to-back.)*

> *(THE WAITER enters.)*

THE WAITER. I'm afraid to say…we are out of the fish. That because of an earlier car accident the casualty was the Red Snapper. I'm sorry to say.

> *(Beat.)*

There was a bend, a turn, the fog, the headlights – blinking, a scream, somebody screamed –

> *(To LUCY.)*

Perhaps you?

LUCY. I'm not –

THE WAITER. Then the plunge and the rocks and the water. So, no Red Snapper tonight which, is too bad because the chef was prepared to do all sorts of things with butter and capers and small, no, *fingerling* potatoes and rosemary or thyme or salt or something. But, because of the earlier car accident all I can offer you are Minty Lamb Sliders. That's the special. Other tables seem to be enjoying them –

LUCY. When was the accident –

THE WAITER. Earlier. *After.* She was leaving The Convention, on her way to dinner I suppose, or it was dinner time or. *You know.* Always in a rush these days. Oh look at that scarf, you have a nice scarf. Reminds me of the scarf they found near the car – the purples and roses and hues and such. A spectrum –

> *(Getting angry.)*

Just…a spectrum of color…

> *(And angrier.)*

I hate when we are out of the fish.

> *(Barely controlled rage.)*

I'm sorry.

> *(***THE WAITER*** *makes to run off…but kinda lurks as waiters sometimes do.)*
>
> *(***LUCY*** *is engrossed in her large menu.)*
>
> *(***NICK*** *turns to* ***ROGER.****)*

NICK. Hey, you.

> *(Tentatively,* ***ROGER*** *half turns to him.)*

Have you ever had the waffles here?

ROGER. Here?

NICK. The dinner waffles.

ROGER. Oh, the *dinner* waffles.

NICK. With the chicken.

ROGER. Right, right. Not –

(**THE WAITER** *is passing by at this exact moment and says the rest in unison with* **ROGER.**)

ROGER.	**THE WAITER.**
– the breakfast waffles with the bacon.	– the breakfast waffles with the bacon.

ROGER. I'm not, how do you say it...I'm not great with *bones.* They're a...problem for me. Looks good though.

(**NICK** *is personally offended.*)

NICK. *"Looks good"?*

ROGER. Looks, ah, delicious.

NICK. *"Looks, ah, delicious"?*
Jesus Christ.

ROGER. Hey –

NICK. *Get-a load-a.*

ROGER. – actually, since you're here, do you mind if I ask? I'm asking about careers.

(**NICK** *is personally offended.*)

NICK. "What's my career?"

ROGER. Exactly. A study-survey. Detailing careers mainly.

NICK. My career *is personal.*

ROGER. What about love?

NICK. Love?

ROGER. There's a situation. I'm dealing with it? I'm dealing with it. But there's a level of uncertainty that...plagues me.

NICK. I'm a percentages guy. You know?

ROGER. Definitely.

NICK. I'm an, "odds are" kinda man.

ROGER. I *definitely* have some percentage guys in my family.

NICK. Odds are, you do.

ROGER. In like, my extended family.

NICK. Hey buddy, tell me something.

ROGER. Space has opened up.

NICK. What's it like?

ROGER. Air has more meaning.

NICK. I remember that.

ROGER. It's like –

>   *(Holding his hands out and up.)*

– my hands are numb.

>   *(**NICK** holds the small chain.)*

NICK. I'm doing this because, I see myself in you.

>   *(**NICK** gives **ROGER** the small chain.)*

ROGER. Ah, a small chain?

NICK. It's from the Titanic.

ROGER. That's…*outstanding.*

NICK. Give her the chain.

ROGER. *Give* her the chain.

NICK. Give her the chain.

ROGER. Imagine that.

NICK. Tell her where it's from.

ROGER. It's from the Titanic.

NICK. Official Artifact.

ROGER. It's an Official Artifact?

NICK. It was in the bathroom. The tub. Kept the water… full.

ROGER. First Class I bet.

NICK. Sure.

ROGER. Official Artifact?

>   *(Beat.)*

NICK. *Yes.*

***

>   *(**LUCY** and **DAPHNE** are washing their hands in the bathroom. Strangely, their movements are*

perfectly in sync with each other. They are both fastidious about really washing well. They totally both wear the same purple scarf.)

LUCY. Excuse me? I believe...do we have the same purple scarf?

DAPHNE. How odd.

LUCY. It looks beautiful on you.

DAPHNE. It was my mother's.

LUCY. Mine too.

Do you think...

(Beat.)

DAPHNE. That we have the same mother?

LUCY. Probably / not.

DAPHNE. Probably not.

(LUCY *realizes this is a moment she can practice generosity.)*

LUCY. They're...out of the Snapper.

(Indicates "outside the bathroom.")

Out there.

The Red Snapper.

DAPHNE. I know.

LUCY. I was just, *sharing* that information with you.

DAPHNE. Amazing, thank you.

LUCY. I've never really liked *trough sinks.*

(DAPHNE *looks both directions at the invisible trough sink.)*

DAPHNE. This *is* a pretty *long trough sink.*

LUCY. Right?

DAPHNE. I'm actually not a fan of the word "trough" at all.

LUCY. I'm not sure that's the exact architectural term for the, for the sink.

DAPHNE. For the trough sink.

LUCY. Yeah.

I think –

Hey, they're out of paper towels.

DAPHNE. Mother fucker.

I'm sure they are.

LUCY. Are you okay?

DAPHNE. What?

LUCY. You seem *agitated*.

DAPHNE. …Add it to the list. I have to wipe my wet hands on my *clothes*. Fuck my hands.

> (**LUCY** *says something inaudible.*)

What?

LUCY. You can…

You can wipe your hands on me.

DAPHNE. What are you talking about.

LUCY. I don't mind. These pants are stupid.

DAPHNE. I'm not…

LUCY. I mean it. I wouldn't have offered.

> (**DAPHNE** *is holding up her annoyingly wet hands, now facing* **LUCY***. She's trying to decide both where to wipe her hands on* **LUCY** *and if she should do it at all.*)

This is / great.

DAPHNE. Isn't this diner / terrible?

LUCY. I think it's kinda wonderful.

***

> (*There is the sound of a car accident. A swirl of movement.*)

> (*The* **DOCTOR/WAITERS** *enter.*)

DOCTOR/WAITER ONE. Things we know include:

DOCTOR/WAITER TWO. There's been an accident –

DOCTOR/WAITER THREE. A curve ball –

DOCTOR/WAITER FOUR. Major blood.

DOCTOR/WAITER TWO. Limbs –

DOCTOR/WAITER ONE. Fins –

DOCTOR/WAITER TWO. Confusion –

DOCTOR/WAITER FOUR. It was dark –

DOCTOR/WAITER ONE. Raining –

DOCTOR/WAITER THREE. No one saw it coming, the curve –

DOCTOR/WAITER ONE. Fish all over the road –

DOCTOR/WAITER THREE. No one found the body –

DOCTOR/WAITER TWO. Not *her* fault for example –

DOCTOR/WAITER THREE. It was just one of those things –

DOCTOR/WAITER TWO. That happens –

DOCTOR/WAITER THREE. Like black ice –

DOCTOR/WAITER TWO. Soft soil –

DOCTOR/WAITER ONE. Erosion –

DOCTOR/WAITER TWO. Time travel?

DOCTOR/WAITER THREE. They could have called –

DOCTOR/WAITER ONE. Someone should have called the restaurant –

DOCTOR/WAITER TWO. The phone kept ringing –

DOCTOR/WAITER THREE. That was a terrible way to find out –

DOCTOR/WAITER ONE. Reservations for parties of six or more.

DOCTOR/WAITER FOUR. Only.

DOCTOR/WAITER THREE. They're not sure it was an accident?

DOCTOR/WAITER ONE. Time travel *involved* –

DOCTOR/WAITER FOUR. A casualty of science –

DOCTOR/WAITER TWO. An unfortunate bit / of timing?

DOCTOR/WAITER ONE. I've just confirmed –

ALL. It was an unfortunate bit of timing.

> (**ETHAN** *emerges from the pack and lingers as the rest exit.*)

(He watches **ROGER** *and* **LUCY** *from a distance while pretending to read silently from his book* The Car Accident.*)*

***

*(***LUCY** *and* **ROGER**, *at the Convention Center, are sitting much closer together.)*

LUCY. You're sure you're not missing something?

ROGER. I have a few minutes.

LUCY. You're going to be astonishing.

ROGER. I have some things for you.

(He pulls out a small bag.)

Nothing big...

Some rocks...

A deer horn letter opener...

These iron-on patches...

*(***LUCY** *looks away.)*

LUCY. A deer horn letter opener?

*(***LUCY** *looks back at* **ROGER**.*)*

ROGER. My uncle's.

LUCY. Now mine?

ROGER. Now yours.

LUCY. Why are you, why are you giving away all your earthly possessions?

ROGER. You just looked like you could really use a solid –

LUCY. I could.

ROGER. Sturdy –

LUCY. I do.

ROGER. – well-cared for deer horn letter opener.

LUCY. Thank you.

(She hesitates...then reaches into her bag.)

Let me see if I have –

ROGER. I don't want anything.

LUCY. I'm sure I –

ROGER. That's not why I gave it to you.

LUCY. – have something –

ROGER. I don't need this to be like a swap meet or –

LUCY. Got it.

ROGER. *(Eager.)* Yeah?

LUCY. It's not as cool as your gift, or, gifts, but maybe you'll like it.

> *(She hesitates only briefly, then hands him a book called* The Car Accident *by Ethan Cambabert.)*

ROGER. *The Car Accident?*

LUCY. It's really good.

ROGER. I bet you read a lot.

LUCY. I read it in a day.

ROGER. I bet you like danger.

LUCY. It's barely even about a car accident.

ROGER. Good.

LUCY. It's like time travel and true love and shootouts. I don't want to give anything away… I'll stop talking. The only thing I'll say is that it's really important to just keep reading it.

Even if at first you think it's not for you.

It is.

It's exactly for you.

ROGER. Hey, it's like we're in a book / club now.

LUCY. Ha, wanna get tattoos?

> *(Beat.)*

ROGER. No /

Not really.

LUCY. I'm joking.

I don't even like tattoos,

Or, just…the one.

(**ROGER** *is looking at the book, and even though it's not a comic book, he likes it.*)

ROGER. *The Car Accident.* I like it.

***

(**ETHAN** *is reading.*)

(*The rain has cleared.*)

ETHAN. "Lucy quietly believed there was a revolution coming.

In the saying that 'the revolutionary makes the revolution,' and she was willing to become one. She believed she was *situationally aware* and by remaining open to all possibility, logically, would have her choice when it came down to picking sides, finding allegiances, and ultimately, one day, perhaps fighting for her life …she always saw herself through someone else's eyes, which is why selfishness came easy. Her slight removal from her true self, made it feel like she was sharing each time she was kind to…herself. She's always been her own best friend, but something in Roger's eyes disrupted this…like slamming a shoulder against the wall to pop the bone back in the joint. The sharp pain was swift, but she could see how reaching across the table for her water glass would be so much easier, and she had never been thirstier…"

(*A shift.*)

(*Something is different.*)

(*Time passes in a strange way, spanning years.*)

(**DAPHNE** *is in her office, looking at papers, doing something important.*)

(**ETHAN** *enters dressed as a Pizza Delivery Guy and carrying a Pizza Box.*)

ETHAN. Here I am...I'm here with your pizza...Pizza. Here.

> (**DAPHNE** *does not look up.*)

> (**ETHAN** *clears his throat a little.*)

Did someone order a PIZZA?

> (**DAPHNE** *glances up, then back down at her important papers.*)

> (**ETHAN** *inches toward her.*)

Hey... Are you...in charge here?

> (*He casually tosses the pizza box aside.*)

You look like you're in charge. Have that sort of, look, about you. I ask because I am interested in the publishing industry and –

DAPHNE. Excuse me?

ETHAN. I've written a book –

DAPHNE. I didn't order a pizza –

ETHAN. It's structurally intense, an Exploded View, a car accident, a love story. It becomes a Western and ends with a shootout –

DAPHNE. How did you get in here?

ETHAN. – I'm bending time, extending a metaphor. There might be a car accident. A duel. There will be guns and rocking chairs and steaming cups of black coffee. It all ends with a death. It's all the same in the end.

DAPHNE. Is there even a pizza in that box?

ETHAN. No –

Wait, I know about you.

I've followed your career. You're a *top* editor.

I know you like experimental authors, like your martinis up and dry.

Enjoy long baths and weekends near a beach...by a pool...you like to be...

surrounded

by

water.

(DAPHNE is intrigued in spite of herself.)

(She opens the pizza box. There IS a pizza in it.)

(She removes a slice and takes a bite.)

DAPHNE. What's your book called?

ETHAN. It's called *The Shootout* –

DAPHNE. What's it about?

ETHAN. A car accident.

DAPHNE. You should call it *The Car Accident.*

ETHAN. It's called *The Car Accident.*

DAPHNE. It should end with a shootout.

ETHAN. I like it!

DAPHNE. How DID you get IN here?

ETHAN. It's really an epic love story about two people meeting for the very first time. Sharing a meal, dropping a chopstick, they have problems...articulating. They become focused on the carpet, a small chain and, finally, a piece of paper, folded up near the plant. Is it garbage? Is it everything –

DAPHNE. I don't like spiders –

ETHAN. – it's exactly like how a spider will walk across the floor so *slowly* and then right when you see it, it pauses. You know?

DAPHNE. I don't like spiders, but I do like the idea that they've been together too long, are sick of each other, the end of a relationship happening at the exact same time as the beginning –

ETHAN. Yes. That happens in my book.

DAPHNE. I thought so.

(She pulls a martini out of her purse and sips it. She loves it.)

Do we care about them?

ETHAN. Yes. Right?

DAPHNE. Absolutely *imperative.*

ETHAN. And there's the whole part where he refuses to order the waffles –

DAPHNE. He gets those disgusting home fries. Yes.

(She laughs girlishly.)

The *tension* in that scene…

You really captured a moment Ethan.

ETHAN. Well, I felt like it was *imperative* to provide a base, a tapestry, a foundation, and a setting for what was coming next. That if he had just *ordered* the waffles people, the "reader," wouldn't have been TIPPED OFF that this day was different than the others.

DAPHNE. This day is special.

ETHAN. I really took your advice that it needed to be apparent from the beginning that this day was "The Day." That's where the whole idea for The Convention came from –

(DAPHNE is so damn pleased.)

DAPHNE. And you never even find out which one she is at!

ETHAN. You…really have an effect on me. Your advice –

DAPHNE. Choices should clearly be made for the sake of story –

ETHAN. And clarity –

DAPHNE. And reveal.

ETHAN. Touché.

(DAPHNE giggles.)

DAPHNE. I spit out a skittle when I read that ROGER was dressed as the Silver Surfer.

ETHAN. You're the comic fan.

DAPHNE. If I had a nickel for every time Galactus swallowed a planet, I'd own a chain of Planet Hollywoods. I mean – who am I?

(She imitates the Silver Surfer.)

ETHAN. No idea.

DAPHNE. I used to pretend I lived on Zenn-La, would call
      myself Shalla-Bal. Did you know the Silver Surfer's
      mother and father killed themselves?

ETHAN. Ha! That's rich!

DAPHNE. That Galactus is bigger than Universes?

      (ETHAN *is scribbling notes.*)

That he consumes worlds?

      (ETHAN *writes that down.*)

ETHAN. *Consumes...worlds...*

DAPHNE. That the Silver Surfer wields the Power Cosmic?
      No wonder he couldn't ever be comfortable in one
      place, it –

ETHAN. *Zenn-La.*

DAPHNE. I mean, what would it take for you to keep
      traveling –

ETHAN. Where am I going –

DAPHNE. – finding worlds for your captor to eat so your
      home planet wouldn't be destroyed and with it your
      own True Love?

ETHAN. It would actually take a lot.

      (*Sets his notebook down and touches her hair.*)

Well, this is all definitely one reason I'm a writer.

DAPHNE. ?

ETHAN. If you really want to know, fine, I'll tell you, it's
      a simple story, amusing, okay, here we go: I wanted to
      be a doctor, but my mother wanted me to be a waiter.
      I want to learn about the heart, she wants me to serve
      artichoke hearts with a garlic aioli dipping sauce. I
      eventually caved and found the best restaurant in town:
      I walked in and am like, "I want to be a waiter. *Here.*"
      And he's like, "You have no experience."
      And I looked him in the eye and am like, "Okay man,
      I'll be a busser."
      And he's like "No."

And I'm like "I will be a dishwasher."
And he's like "No."
And I'm like "Okay – I'll be a FREE dishwasher"
And he's like…"No."

    *(**DAPHNE** moves closer to him.)*

DAPHNE. That's a beautiful story.

ETHAN. I don't tell that to many people…

DAPHNE. So you became a writer.

ETHAN. It never would have happened without your encouragement, Daphne.

DAPHNE. No, it was you. Your persistence.

ETHAN. Your enthusiasm –

DAPHNE. Your cool hair –

    *(**ETHAN** smiles.)*

ETHAN. That Pizza.

    (They share a laugh.)

DAPHNE. How did you ever? Where did you come up with such a thing?

ETHAN. You'll never believe me.

DAPHNE. *(Strangely flirting.)* Oh Ethan –
you…
know…
I…will.

ETHAN. I was at a convention.

DAPHNE. Like in the book?

    (During the following they become physically intertwined. Each amazed at the other's body, how it feels, how it moves. It's almost as if they are floating weightlessly in Space.)

ETHAN. Before the book, in real life, after you left Zenn-La.

DAPHNE. *(Purr-ing it.)* Zennnn-La –

ETHAN. There was a presentation by: A Man. He spoke for hours and hours on the subject of life, of love, of How To Get Into Buildings. There was fire, images, music. There was something strangely intriguing about him. There actually was a fire, so I never heard the end of his speech but I *trusted* him. There was a sadness behind his eyes but a fierceness to his cadence – he inspired *and* endeared.

DAPHNE. He was talking about Pizza?

ETHAN. No.

It's always about a uniform, isn't it? He spoke about the uniform of a Pizza Delivery Guy.

About its potential. He spoke, and I listened.

(They kiss.)

***

(A transformation occurs: The reveal of a screen… the re-arranging of the space…Perhaps **ETHAN** *vacuums…It's that weird balance of preparations for something either sad or important or both. This should take a good minute or two before* **ROGER** *appears…)*

***

(A Title slide is projected – HOW TO GET INTO BUILDINGS.)

*(***ROGER*** looks different then before. Slicker. His hair's wet. Combed back. He's nervous.)*

(He holds a clicker that advances the slides [but it sounds like a gun when he clicks it.])

(The lights dim and **LUCY** *is watching – unnoticed.)*

ROGER. Good afternoon Ladies and Gentlemen, Superheroes, and Lords of the Underworld...

After last year's pyrotechnical glitch, I've decided this year to give my presentation in the very simple Power Point form. Less bling, more safety. If you'd like, I can email this file on afterward and you can share it, or give the presentation yourself, to, or, with friends or loved ones or family members, or with co-workers or grandparents – just anyone!

> *(He pulls out a small tape recorder, sets it next to him, and hits play.)*
>
> *(We faintly hear Survivor's* **"MOMENT OF TRUTH"** *from the first* Karate Kid *movie underscoring his presentation – the audio only coming from the tape recorder. Occasionally* **ROGER** *will pause in his presentation when there is a particularly good line he likes and he'll sing along, then return to what he is saying. If the song runs out, the next song on the tape is Peter Cetera* **"GLORY OF LOVE,"** *from* The Karate Kid Part II, *until the end.*)*
>
> *(***ROGER** *advances the slide – BANG, the first slide appears.)*
>
> *(The slide is an image of the Empire State Building.)*
>
> *(He holds his first note card.)*

---

* A license to produce *How To Get Into Buildings* does not include a performance license for "Moment of Truth," "Glory of Love," or any songs from *The Karate Kid* and *The Karate Kid Part II*. The publisher and author suggest that the licensee contact ASCAP or BMI to ascertain the music publisher and contact such music publisher to license or acquire permission for performance of the songs. If a license or permission is unattainable for "Moment of Truth" or "Glory of Love," the licensee may not use the songs in *How To Get Into Buildings* but may create original compositions in a similar style. For further information, please see Music Use Note on page 3.

What people, today, in our society, on Earth, don't realize is, that most buildings are just that: *Buildings*. They are buildings with *people* in them. You, or One, may, for instance, *just walk in the door.* Just go into a building and say:

"Hey is the superintendent around?"

And they're like, "What?"

And you say, more forcefully, *"Hey – is the super here?"*

And sometimes they say, "No, come back after lunch."

And you should just say "cool" or something and just hang out for a bit, outside or at Starbucks, and then, go back after lunch and start it all again.

Persistence.

> (**ROGER** *advances the slide – BANG, the second slide appears.*)

> (*It's a pie chart, split into three sections, denoting different careers – Pizza Delivery Guy, Doctor, Waiter.*)

> (*He now holds his second note card.*)

ROGER. You may think you know what you want to "study" or "be" but I'm telling you right now, don't go running around like a child saying "I'm going to be a Doctor when I grown up." Because you'll be lucky if you're a Waiter. *Lucky.*

So, Stop speculating everyone! You know?

Right now you're all just *speculating.*

Speculating.

> (**ROGER** *advances the slide – BANG, the third slide appears.*)

> (*It's an exploded view donut chart charting the population of the World split into three sections – Land, Sea, Water.*)

> (*He now holds his third note card.*)

The great thing that I was never told, and that I wish I knew at a much younger age, is this:

The world is just a bunch of people dude.

You just have to be ready to BE one of them.

And you can be annoying or persistent – that's totally fine!

> (**ROGER** *advances the slide – BANG, the fourth slide appears.*)
>
> (*It's four quadrants, in each – a pizza, the Empire State building, a pizza box, the entrance to the building.*)
>
> (*He now holds his fourth note card.*)

ROGER. One way modern men, and women, meet people is to dress as a common Pizza Delivery Guy, or Gal, and enter a building. Tips to ensure entrance include: Make sure you carry the pizza box as if there is a pizza inside.

People, apparently, will let someone with a Pizza in ANYWHERE.

"I'm here to see Mr. Carmichael on the twenty-first floor."

"Go right up."

"Nancy from accounting ordered a deep dish Hawaiian, which floor is she on again?"

"Eleven. Lucky Nancy!"

Whether there's a pizza actually IN the box or not, that's up to you. *Because you are just a dude trying to figure out a way into a building.* Into a club. It's one big club, and with persistence, if you stop speculating, and if you show up ready to deliver a pizza, you'll have a fair chance of getting in.

> (**ROGER** *advances the slide – BANG, the fifth slide appears.*)
>
> (*The outline of nine empty boxes, the images will build when he mentions each item.*)
>
> (*He now holds his fifth note card.*)

(If it hasn't come on already, **ROGER** *switches at this point to Peter Cetera's "GLORY OF LOVE," from* The Karate Kid Part II.*)

ROGER. So, be sure you show up with a pizza box –

(A stylish pizza delivery person pic fills the first box.)

– and get ready for a waterfall effect or snowball effect of life's big elements to start happening to you.
They'll be like:
Grab a chair!

(Chair pic fills a box.)

There's your desk!

(Desk pic fills a box.)

Here's your cool new cards!

(Cool business cards pic fills a box.)

That's your phone!

(Phone pic fills box.)

Meet your wife!

(Hot wife pic fills box.)

There's your kids!

(Sweet kids pic fills box.)

Board meeting at noon!

(Board meeting pic fills box.)

Last one to the diner has to buy!

---

* A license to produce *How To Get Into Buildings* does not include a performance license for "Glory of Love." The publisher and author suggest that the licensee contact ASCAP or BMI to ascertain the music publisher and contact such music publisher to license or acquire permission for performance of the song. If a license or permission is unattainable for "Glory of Love" the licensee may not use the song in *How To Get Into Buildings* but may create an original composition in a similar style. For further information, please see Music Use Note on page 3.

(Diner pic fills box.)

ROGER. Now look at you. You're in the building, in the club, hell you're on your way to being *President-of-the-Club.* I for one, couldn't be more proud because it's an *awful* world out there, but look at you.

You just made it.

You made it.

Thank you.

> *(Wild applause.)*
>
> *(He sees **LUCY** in the crowd and smiles.)*

***

> **(DAPHNE** *and* **ETHAN** *are eating California rolls out of a Bento Box.)*
>
> *(The sound of rain.)*

DAPHNE. As long as it makes sense –

ETHAN. It makes sense.

DAPHNE. As long as it sounds good –

ETHAN. Parallels. Like you. Take YOU. Let's take you for example.

DAPHNE. No, no, no –

ETHAN. You're recently divorced –

DAPHNE. Ha, I see you –

ETHAN. How long has it been since you and Nick –

DAPHNE. I see what you're doing –

ETHAN. What?

DAPHNE. I *know* what you're doing –

ETHAN. I'm simply –

DAPHNE. "What? I'm simply –"

Uh-huh. *No way.* Don't put me in it.

> *(He's quiet for a moment.)*

ETHAN. Don't be mad –

DAPHNE. *Ethan Cambabert –*

ETHAN. Just hear me out –

DAPHNE. Ok. Wow.

ETHAN. Daph – I love you –

DAPHNE. Stop –

ETHAN. It's really romantic.

DAPHNE. My divorce?

ETHAN. I've tried to really capture it. Artistically.

DAPHNE. *What?*

ETHAN. I've looked for the beauty in it and I think you'll be happy with what I've managed to do. I'm clever –

DAPHNE. You're terrible.

ETHAN. There are pistols.

> (**DAPHNE** *perks up a bit.*)

DAPHNE. I'm listening.

ETHAN. You and Nick *know* it's over but decide that it's too easy to just –

> (*Does stupid "air quotes."*)

"Walk away." We need to feel it's final. A sacrifice. So, you decide to end it. A duel. With pistols –

DAPHNE. Back to back –

ETHAN. Back to back, pistols at dawn –

DAPHNE. Counting down from ten –

ETHAN. Pacing it out –

DAPHNE. I'm quicker than he is.

I have smaller hands –

My finger fits better cradling the trigger –

I have better instincts –

I hear faster than him –

See farther than him –

I have less *bacteria* on my skin.

Less then he does.

My hands are cleaner.

> (*She sneezes.*)

ETHAN. Bless –

DAPHNE. When I go to pull the trigger I don't bring all the shame and self-pity that he does.

So in that regard,

I'm lighter.

I weigh *less.*

Emotionally.

Which makes me quicker in the release.

ETHAN. All of that was taken into consideration –

DAPHNE. I hope you also noted my love of American Westerns –

A well-placed underscore –

I like a good narration –

Short sentences –

But not too short –

A crowd hovering around –

People watching –

I'm always better, just *better* with people watching than with no one watching –

I'm more likely to achieve what I've set out to do if I know I'm being, being, what is it?

Right – being unfairly judged by a small, no by a *tiny*, no by a *small* crowd of strangers.

ETHAN. Exactly!

DAPHNE. ETHAN!

> (**DAPHNE** *is extremely happy! Why had nobody ever before told her she could take control of her own life so suddenly and completely? Wow, she's euphoric.*)

Did you know about this? That this could happen, that just saying goodbye, walking out the door, loading the gun, unloading the gun, loading the gun, taking aim and shooting, that things would ultimately FEEL SO GOOD? I mean, talk about RELEASE. It's dangerous.

> (*This is contagious;* **ETHAN** *is so fucking pleased with himself.*)

ETHAN. I thought it might happen.

DAPHNE. *Damn.*

ETHAN. *Damn!*

DAPHNE. I've always wanted to kill someone in a shootout.

***

(A phone rings and **LUCY** *tries to find where it's coming from…Oh, it's just a really tiny phone that's been hanging around her neck on a chain like a necklace. She holds it up to her ear.)*

LUCY. First time caller speaking…

…It's me, long time listener.

…Are you there?

MRS. REINHARDT. Yes, I'm here –

LUCY. I've been on hold…hello?

MRS. REINHARDT. I've been with other customers –

LUCY. But it's me, eleven dollars a month?

I was wondering if you could let me know if this is the correct choice.

MRS. REINHARDT. For eleven dollars a month I am not able to say –

LUCY. Oh –

MRS. REINHARDT. I'm only able to let you know that for a pledge of twenty-five dollars you'll receive a brick with your name on it. For one hundred dollars we can fix the oxidization on the left hand. For eleven dollars all I can offer is a small key with no instructions. There will be a hole in the key – you're encouraged to put a chain through the hole. You're encouraged to wear the key around your neck, a collar, in the hopes that one day you will encounter a small lock.

(Beat.)

Hold please –

(Hold music comes on. But only for a moment.)

There was a bend –

LUCY. Hey! Hey... I'm willing to make a *larger* donation.

MRS. REINHARDT. A turn, the fog, the headlights –

LUCY. I'm aware there are *costs* involved.

MRS. REINHARDT. No one saw it coming, the curve –

> *(There is a choppiness now to the connection on* **MRS. REINHARDT**'s *part.)*

LUCY.
If I'm willing to make a larger donation would, what would be possible? I *am* willing to make a larger donation. I fully understand the risk involved and already have the chain. For that key. How much of the oxidation could be cleared up? What would it take –

MRS. REINHARDT.
It should be there in thirty minutes or less or your money back... Guaranteed... I'm – connection – left knee – artichoke heart – blinking.

> *(Click.)*

*** *** ***

> *(***LUCY*** waits impatiently for ***ROGER***. She practices complimenting him.)*

LUCY. You were astonishing!

You were –

You were everything!

You captured a moment.

You –

I love Hawaiian Pizza.

Ha! You were...

> *(He arrives, glowing from his presentation.)*

That was –

ROGER. Yeah?

LUCY. Like, I don't know where to start.

ROGER. Did you take a lot of notes?

LUCY. What?

ROGER. A lot of people take notes? At conventions?

LUCY.	**ROGER.**
Oh right. No. But I... I'm not a note taker. But that doesn't mean I wasn't listening or anything.	Oh, right, naw, totally.

LUCY. I think *you*, potentially, changed a lot of lives in there. Just now. I don't know about anyone else, and maybe I mean, you maybe just changed *mine*, but I feel...

(She holds her hands up.)

My hands feel a little numb?

I have a strong...

I am more, *willing?*

ROGER. There's only one way to find out.

(Beat.)

LUCY. Have you read it yet?

ROGER. The –

LUCY. The book.

ROGER. But, I just –

LUCY. I didn't know if you were...a speed-reader.

(Beat.)

You're probably not there yet or anything, but turn to page three-hundred-and-thirty-three.

*(**ETHAN** enters, wearing his white waiter apron, a spray bottle in one pocket, and carries a plant watering can.)*

(He eyes them a little bit, but they don't notice.)

(He hovers near a plant: occasionally spraying its leaves.)

ROGER. *(Reading.)* "Then the daggers and swords melt together
and there are two pistols sitting in front of them,
a salt and pepper shaker,
a spoon suspended in air,
a tower of sugar in between.
Maybe a crumpled up napkin,
her fork,
his knife,
the ketchup cap.
Both of them staring at the pistol they have secretly chosen for themselves,
knowing they will end up how they always end up –
Isolated in time, unaware of the shift.
Seemingly content but ultimately unsatisfied.
A breeze, some dust, that woman in the rocking chair."

> *(**LUCY** reads the rest of the line with him.)*

ROGER & LUCY. "Daphne calmly pushes up the puffy sleeves on her barmaid's dress, assuring she won't snag her thumb on the fabric when her hand rushes to her side. They walk toward each other, then pivot."

> *(Focus is shifting... **ETHAN** gradually takes over from **ROGER**. **LUCY** slips away...)*

ETHAN & ROGER. "They are now back to back
trying their best to breathe normal.
Nick ignores the urge to run
his fingers through his hair one last time."

> *(**ROGER** and **LUCY** stare into each other's eyes as **ETHAN** thoroughly sprays the plant during the following.)*

ETHAN. "Electric and terrifying, dreamlike, but more real than what they have known before.

They each sense the pulling distraction of the other, recognize the inability to block out the feeling of warmth they sense from the body behind them.

His left shoulder burning her right as they barely touch.

Everything disappearing –

The diner,

The table,

The coffee,

The rain,

Only to be replaced by

The dirt road,

The old bar,

The horses,

A sheriff,

The breaking dawn.

And the pistols.

The steel in their hands growing cold as they count down, backwards from ten.

Ten.

Nine –"

>   (**ETHAN** *wanders off.*)

LUCY. Okay, you can stop there.

>   (*They are quiet for a minute.*)

ROGER. I'm not sure –

LUCY. You do.

ROGER. So, they love each other / but they shoot each other?

LUCY. Have you ever made a donation and got your name on a brick?

ROGER. But are they at a diner or on that hill or in, like, a ghost town?

>   (**LUCY** *smiles.*)

LUCY. I think so.

ROGER. They just let it all happen?

LUCY. It's about a lot of things.

> *(The rest of the **DOCTOR/WAITERS** enter, looking kinda like Convention Center Maintenance Employees.)*

> *(They merge with **ETHAN** and all carry plant watering cans. Auspiciously, they huddle around a nearby plant, sneaking looks at **LUCY** and **ROGER** as they all water the plants again.)*

DOCTOR/WAITER ONE. Things we know include:

DOCTOR/WAITER TWO. They closed the highway –

DOCTOR/WAITER THREE. Traffic diverted –

DOCTOR/WAITER FOUR. Helicopters.

DOCTOR/WAITER TWO. Pepperoni –

DOCTOR/WAITER ONE. Pineapple –

DOCTOR/WAITER TWO. *Kalamata* Olives –

DOCTOR/WAITER FOUR. Organ donor?

DOCTOR/WAITER ONE. Pesto?!

DOCTOR/WAITER THREE. No one saw it coming / the curve –

DOCTOR/WAITER ONE. More water –

DOCTOR/WAITER THREE. More time –

DOCTOR/WAITER TWO. More sauce please –

DOCTOR/WAITER THREE. No substitutions –

DOCTOR/WAITER TWO. No *pesto* please –

DOCTOR/WAITER THREE. *Red* sauce –

DOCTOR/WAITER TWO. *Extra* sauce –

DOCTOR/WAITER ONE. No *onions* please –

DOCTOR/WAITER TWO. No *guns* please –

DOCTOR/WAITER THREE. Nice c*rust* –

DOCTOR/WAITER ONE. We'll have the *Power Cosmic* –

DOCTOR/WAITER TWO. With the olives –

DOCTOR/WAITER THREE. The *kalamata* olives –

DOCTOR/WAITER ONE. *Crispy crust* please.

DOCTOR/WAITER FOUR. Hold please.

(Beat. Brief hold Muzak.)

DOCTOR/WAITER THREE. Hold the / Red Snapper please

DOCTOR/WAITER ONE. We're out of fish please.

DOCTOR/WAITER FOUR. Water to survive –

DOCTOR/WAITER TWO. More / water –?

DOCTOR/WAITER ONE. / I've just confirmed more / water is necessary –

DOCTOR/WAITER THREE. Oh yes, more water.

DOCTOR/WAITER FOUR. Water no / ice please. Water is necess –

ALL. Water is necessary.

> *(They are done watering and leave.)*
>
> *(**DOCTOR/WAITER FOUR** drops a small, folded-up piece of paper as they exit.)*

ROGER. That was a pretty aggressive plant watering squad.

> *(**ROGER** picks up the folded-up piece of paper and reads it.)*

LUCY. What does it say?

ROGER. This is interesting –

LUCY. What –

ROGER. It says I LOVE YOU.

> *(**LUCY** is unsure where to look; definitely **ROGER** is no longer an option.)*

LUCY. Does it?

ROGER. No…

> *(**LUCY** looks at **ROGER** again.)*

LUCY. Oh.

ROGER. It says IF YOU'RE READING THIS YOU'RE ALREADY DEAD.

LUCY. It does?

ROGER. No… It says CLOSE YOUR EYES AND HOLD ON TIGHT AND STOP QUESTIONING AND JUST BE

> *(**LUCY** likes that.)*

LUCY. Cool –

ROGER. Actually –

LUCY. – fortune.

ROGER. – it's a receipt for a burrito. From the Burrito Barn.

***

(Everything changes.)

*(****ETHAN****, wearing a cool cowboy hat, is reading from the last pages of his book.)*

*(****NICK**** and ****DAPHNE**** enter; ****ROGER**** and ****LUCY**** blend into the audience.)*

(The sunset is beautiful and Spaghetti Western-esque music plays until the end.)

ETHAN. "*Chapter Three Hundred and Ninety-Three...Hello* 1881!

After clearing the debris from his eyes, Nick's hand went to his side, annoyed at the mustard stain on his cuff, but immediately relieved at finding the pistol was still there. He gave a cough."

*(****NICK**** coughs.)*

"Wherever he was it was dusty, and dirty and smelled like a cowhide.

Had Daphne made it?

'Daphne?' he called, but quietly.

'Daphne...' he whispered.

A few moments passed

before he heard her saying, barely audibly,

'Over here *you fool.*'

Daphne was wearing a barmaid's dress, low cut so her top spilled out into the martini she stirred slowly with a toothpick. She threw back her head and laughed at the look on Nick's face which said everything that was true: that he hadn't actually expected her to survive the accident, that he was jealous of her beauty, that he confused even himself when forced to face his feelings – he didn't want to live without her, but the sight of her drove him crazy.

He smiled and tipped his hat. Only he wore no hat, so he tipped the air with his fingers."

> (**ETHAN** *opens his book, but wait…the inside of the book is hollow and contains two pistols.*)

> (*It feels clear that things were always going to end this way.*)

"The hesitation was in the body… Both of them knew that this was the only way to end things."

> (**DAPHNE** *selects her pistol.*)

"Both of them knew, that if they looked at each other in the eye for too long they might stop everything. Fall back in love. Be together for eternity."

DAPHNE. She was afraid to think too far back, to when everything was new, to when there was an embarrassing amount of kindness.

> (**ROGER** *takes* **LUCY**'s *hand, it's like they're at a movie now.*)

LUCY. (*A whisper to* **ROGER**.) I've been thinking about the World Population.

ROGER. About Nancy from accounting?

LUCY. About Nancy from accounting.

> (**ROGER** *squeezes her hand.*)

NICK. Nick couldn't decide which moment he stopped seeing, he couldn't pinpoint the last time his base emotion wasn't fueled by the rude, warm feeling of disappointment.

DAPHNE & NICK. (*In mutual recognition!*) That one time, in California, with the peaches and sunburns and then, yeah, rain!

ETHAN. – They know that if they looked at each other in the eye for too long they might

stop everything…
Fall back in love…
Go home…
But neither wanted that.

(**NICK** *takes the other pistol.*)

Too much had happened.

(**MRS. REINHARDT** *arrives with a rocking chair and sits, rocking.*)

Nick would never forgive the way she looked at him and Daphne was too proud to make any sort of necessary adjustment, even if a tiny part of her wondered if they should talk about what they were doing –

(**ETHAN**, *perhaps on mic, continues to read – softly doubling the lines.*)

NICK. She's quicker than me.

DAPHNE. Hey, let's cut our fingers, smear the walls.

NICK. Has smaller hands.

DAPHNE. Hey, I believed in everything.

NICK. Her finger fits better cradling the trigger.

DAPHNE. Hey, have you seen the waiter I really need more water.

NICK. She has better instincts –

DAPHNE. I can't breathe.

NICK. Hears faster than me –

DAPHNE. My hand is numb –

NICK. Sees farther than me –

DAPHNE. Remember the *pine nuts in the tapenade?*

NICK. She has…less bacteria on her skin.

DAPHNE. When I pull the trigger –

NICK. Less than me.

DAPHNE. When I go to pull the trigger.

NICK. Her hands are…cleaner.

DAPHNE. My hands will be cleaner.

NICK. But when I go to pull the trigger I don't bring all the shame and self-pity that she does.

    (**DAPHNE** *is thrown by this.*)

So in that regard,

I am lighter.

She weighs less.

But I weigh less.

Emotionally.

Which makes me quicker on the release.

ETHAN. The time for talk was over – the decisions were made long ago, when no one was looking. The sun was creeping up and the morning was beautiful, cloud parts still hung low in the horizon, the valley refusing to let them go. The moment had come...

MRS. REINHARDT. Usually there is the sound of a horse –

DAPHNE. Dust kicked up?

NICK. Then dust settling –

MRS. REINHARDT. There is dust, for sure.

    (**DAPHNE** *and* **NICK** *are back to back.*)

DAPHNE. The parties then un-mount the horse –

NICK. *Dismount* –

ETHAN. They *dismount* the horse –

MRS. REINHARDT. And someone, a small boy perhaps, ties that horse to a nearby pole.

    (**DAPHNE** *and* **NICK** *are pacing it out.*)

NICK. There's always a pole –

DAPHNE. And a horse –

ETHAN. And a bar –

MRS. REINHARDT. And some dust –

ETHAN. There is a porch –

MRS. REINHARDT. The past in a rocking chair –

ETHAN. She's been here before –

DAPHNE. Seen it before –

NICK. The mother of someone –

ETHAN. The lover of someone –

ALL. That probably died in a shootout.

ETHAN. They arrive –

DAPHNE. Aware of why they're here –

NICK. They have chosen their pistols –

ETHAN. It's / dawn –

DAPHNE. Moments before dawn –

NICK. The pink on the horizon –

DAPHNE. The pink of his skin –

NICK. The skin of his teeth.

> *(**LUCY** sees **MRS. REINHARDT** and raises a hand in recognition.)*

> *(**MRS. REINHARDT** nods.)*

MRS. REINHARDT. Under these circumstance –

ETHAN. Under these circumstances, it's unclear / if –

MRS. REINHARDT. The rules are clear?

ETHAN. This is how it ends.

> *(**DAPHNE** and **NICK** ready themselves.)*

> *(**ROGER** hands **LUCY** some popcorn.)*

> *(**ETHAN**'s doubling of lines has stopped…)*

NICK. The moment / before

DAPHNE. The close up on the / eyes

NICK. The flicker of insecurity

ETHAN & MRS. REINHARDT. The ninth hour.

> *(**ROGER** whispers something to **LUCY** and she laughs.)*

DAPHNE. Hands at the sides.

NICK. Gun on the sides.

DAPHNE. Stretching out the fingers.

NICK. Hands forming fists.

DAPHNE. The metal against the holster.

NICK. The scraping of the leather –
DAPHNE. The steel in the air –
NICK. The outreach of the arm –
DAPHNE. The outreach of the arm –
ETHAN. The outreach of the arm –

   (Blackout.)

ALL. The click of the pistol.

   (Some Cool Music.)

The End